The Little Prince

I believe he escaped by hitching a ride
with a flock of migrating wild birds.

ANTOINE DE SAINT-EXUPÉRY

The Little Prince

ALMA BOOKS

ALMA CLASSICS LTD
Hogarth House
32-34 Paradise Road
Richmond
Surrey TW9 1SE
United Kingdom
www.almaclassics.com

The Little Prince first published in 1943
This translation first published by Alma Classics Ltd in 2015

Translation © Gregory Norminton, 2015
Extra Material © Alma Classics Ltd

Printed and bound by Oriental Press, Dubai

ISBN: 978-1-84749-423-8

The Little Prince

To Léon Werth.

I hope children will forgive me if I dedicate this book to a grown-up. I have a serious excuse: this grown-up is the best friend I have in the world. I have another excuse: this grown-up understands everything, even books for children. I have a third excuse: this grown-up lives in France, where he is cold and hungry. He really needs consoling. If all these excuses aren't enough, I'm happy to dedicate this book to the child whom this grown-up used to be. All grown-ups started out as children. (But few of them remember it.) So I correct my dedication:

To Léon Werth
when he was a little boy.

I

Once, when I was six years old, I saw a marvellous picture in a book on rainforests called *Real-Life Stories*. It depicted a boa constrictor swallowing a wild animal. Here is a replica of the picture.

In the book it said: "Boa constrictors swallow their prey whole, without chewing. Afterwards they cannot move, and sleep for six months digesting."

I thought a great deal about goings-on in the jungle and, in turn, with a crayon, managed to produce my first drawing. My drawing number 1. It was like this:

I showed my masterpiece to the grown-ups and asked them if my drawing frightened them.

They answered: "What's frightening about a hat?"

My drawing was not of a hat. It showed a boa constrictor digesting an elephant. I then drew the insides of the boa constrictor, so that the grown-ups could understand. They're always looking for explanations. My drawing number 2 was like this:

The grown-ups advised me to set drawings of open or closed boa constrictors aside, and to concentrate instead on geography, history, mathematics and grammar. So it was, at the age of six, that I abandoned a magnificent career as a painter. I'd been discouraged by the failure of my drawing number 1 and my drawing number 2. Grown-ups never understand anything on their own, and it's tiring, for children, to be for ever and ever explaining...

Having to choose another profession, I learnt to fly planes. I flew a little all over the world. And it's true that geography served me well. At a glance I could distinguish China from Arizona. That's very useful, if you get lost in the night.

And so, in the course of my life, I've had lots of encounters with lots of serious people. I have lived a great deal among grown-ups. I have seen them up close. It hasn't done much to improve my opinion.

Whenever I met one who seemed faintly perceptive, I subjected them to the experiment with my drawing number 1, which I've always kept. I wanted to know if they could really understand. But they always answered: "It's a hat." So I would tell them nothing about boa constrictors, or rainforests, or the stars. I put myself at their level. I spoke to them about bridge, golf, politics and neckties. And the grown-up was very pleased to know such a reasonable man...

II

And so I lived alone, with no one really to talk to, until a breakdown in the Saharan desert, six years ago. Something had failed in my engine. As I had neither passengers nor a mechanic, I was getting ready to attempt, all on my own, some difficult repairs. It was a matter of life or death. I had scarcely enough drinking water to last eight days.

That first night I went to sleep on the sand a thousand miles from any human dwelling. I was much more alone than a person shipwrecked on a raft in the middle of the ocean. So you can imagine my surprise when, at sunrise, a strange little voice woke me. It said:

"Please... draw me a sheep!"

"Huh!"

"Draw me a sheep..."

I leapt to my feet as if struck by lightning. I rubbed my eyes thoroughly. I had a good look. And I saw an altogether extraordinary little fellow who was watching me with a solemn expression. Here is the best portrait that I was able to make of him, later on. But, of course, my drawing is much less beautiful than the model. It's not my fault. Grown-ups had discouraged me from my artistic career when I was six, and I hadn't learnt to draw anything other than open or closed boa constrictors.

So I was watching this apparition with wide, astonished eyes. Don't forget that I was a thousand miles from any human dwelling. Yet my little fellow looked neither lost, nor dying of weariness, dying of hunger, dying of thirst or dying of fear. He seemed nothing like a child lost in the middle of the desert, a thousand miles from any human dwelling. When at last I managed to speak, I asked him:

"But… what are you doing out here?"

And he said again, very softly, in all seriousness:

"Please… draw me a sheep…"

When a mystery is too overwhelming, you dare not disobey. As absurd as it seemed to me a thousand miles from any human dwelling and in mortal danger, I reached into my pocket for a piece of paper and a pen. Then I remembered that I had studied mostly geography, history, mathematics and grammar, and I said to the little fellow (in something of a bad mood) that I didn't know how to draw. He replied:

"It doesn't matter. Draw me a sheep."

As I had never drawn a sheep, I redid, for his benefit, one of the only two drawings I was capable of. That of the closed boa constrictor. And I was astounded to hear the little man reply:

Here is the best portrait that I was able to make of him, later on.

"No! No! I don't want an elephant inside a boa constrictor. A boa constrictor is dangerous, and an elephant is very bulky. My home's very small. I need a sheep. Draw me a sheep."

So I drew.

He looked carefully, then said:

"No! That one's already very ill. Do another."

I drew:

My friend smiled kindly, indulgently:

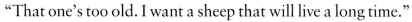

"See for yourself… that's not a sheep, it's a ram. It's got horns…"

So I redid my drawing again:

But it was rejected, like the previous ones:

"That one's too old. I want a sheep that will live a long time."

Finally, my patience at an end, as I was in a hurry to start dismantling my engine, I scribbled this drawing:

And I exclaimed:

"That's the crate. The sheep you want is inside."

But I was very surprised to see my young critic's face light up:

"That's exactly how I wanted it! Do you think this sheep needs a lot of grass?"

"Why?"

"Because my place is very small…"

10

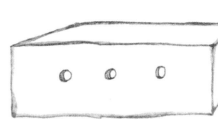

"I'm sure it'll be enough. I've given you a very small sheep."
He bent his head over the drawing:
"Not that small... Look! It's fallen asleep..."
And so it was that I made the acquaintance of the little prince.

III

It took me a long time to understand where he came from. The little prince, who asked me lots of questions, seemed never to hear my own. Little by little, things he said at random revealed everything to me. When, for instance, he saw my plane for the first time (I won't attempt my plane, it's far too complex a drawing) he asked me:

"What's that thing?'

"It's not a thing. It flies. It's a plane. It's my plane."

And I was proud to tell him that I flew. Then he cried out:

"Really! You fell from the sky!"

"Yes," I said modestly.

"Ah! That's funny!..."

And the little prince gave a very pretty laugh that irritated me profoundly. I want my misfortunes to be taken seriously. Then he added:

"So, you also come from the sky! Which planet are you from?"

I saw at once a glimmer of light in the mystery of his presence, and asked bluntly:

"Why, do you come from another planet?"

But he didn't answer. He nodded his head gently while considering my plane:

"It's true that you can't have come from far, on that..."

And he sank into a daydream that lasted a long time. Finally, taking my sheep out of his pocket, he buried himself in contemplation of his treasure.

You can imagine how intrigued I was by this partial revelation about these "other planets". I tried to find out more:

"Where do you come from, my little man? Where is 'home' for you? Where do you want to take my sheep?"

He answered after a thoughtful silence:

"The good thing about the crate you've given me is that it can be its house at night."

"Of course. And if you're good, I'll also give you a rope to tie it up with during the day. And a post."

The suggestion appeared to shock the little prince.

"Tie it up? What a strange idea!"

"If you don't tie it up, it will wander off and get lost."

Again my friend laughed out loud:

"Where do you expect it to go?"

"Anywhere. Straight ahead..."

Then the little prince replied gravely:

The Little Prince on Asteroid B 612

"It doesn't matter, my place is so small!"
And, with a touch perhaps of sadness, he added:
"If you go straight ahead you can't go very far…"

IV

Thus I learnt a second very important thing: that his home planet was scarcely larger than a house.

It didn't surprise me much. I was well aware that, besides the big planets like Earth, Jupiter, Mars and Venus, to which we have given names, there are hundreds of others that are so small that it's hard to see them with a telescope. When an astronomer discovers one of them, he gives it a number for a name. For example he calls it "Asteroid 325".

I have good reasons to believe that the planet the little prince came from is Asteroid B 612. This asteroid was only detected by telescope once, in 1909, by a Turkish astronomer.

He went on to give a major demonstration of his discovery to an

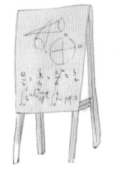

international congress on astronomy. But nobody believed him on account of his outfit. That's what grown-ups are like.

Happily for the reputation of asteroid B 612, a Turkish dictator imposed western dress on his people on pain of death. The astronomer repeated his demonstration in 1920, wearing very elegant clothes. And this time everyone agreed with him.

If I've told you these details about asteroid B 612 and shared its number with you, it's on account of grown-ups. Grown-ups like numbers. When you tell them about a new friend, they never enquire into what matters most. They never say to you: "How does his voice sound? What are his favourite games? Does he collect butterflies?" They ask you: "How old is he? How many brothers has he got? How much does he weigh? How much does his father earn?" Only then do they think they have an idea of him. If you say to grown-ups: "I've seen a beautiful house of pink brick, with geraniums at the windows and doves on the roof..." they can't picture this house. You

have to tell them: "I saw a house worth a hundred thousand francs." At that point they exclaim: "Isn't it pretty!"

Thus, if you say to them: "The proof that the little prince existed is that he was beautiful, that he laughed and he wanted a sheep. When you want a sheep, it's proof that you exist," they will shrug their shoulders and call you a child! But if you say to them: "The planet he came from was Asteroid B 612," then they will be convinced and will spare you their questions. That's how they are. You mustn't resent them for it. Children must be very forbearing towards grown-ups.

But, of course, we who understand life couldn't care less about numbers! I would have liked to have begun this story like a fairy tale. I would have liked to have said:

"Once upon a time there was a little prince who lived on a planet scarcely larger than himself, and who was in need of a friend…" For those who understand life, it would have sounded much more true.

You see, I don't want my book to be read lightly. It pains me so much to relay these memories. It's six years already since my friend went away with his sheep. If I'm trying to describe him here, it's in order not to forget him. It's sad to forget a friend. Not everyone has had a friend. And I might become like the grown-ups who are only interested in numbers. This is why I've bought a box of watercolours and pencils. It's hard to take up drawing again, at my age, when you've only ever attempted open and closed boa constrictors at the age of six. I will, of course, try to draw the best likenesses I can. But I'm not entirely sure that I'll succeed. One drawing works and another looks nothing like him. I'm not quite getting his size. Here the little prince is too tall. There he's too short. I'm also unsure about the colour of his outfit. And so I feel my way as best I can. I will also make mistakes on more important details. You'll have to forgive me. My friend never explained anything. Maybe he thought I was like him. But alas, I cannot see sheep through crates. Perhaps I am a bit like the grown-ups. I must have aged.

V

Each day I learnt something about the planet, about his departure and his journey. The information came out slowly, through occasional remarks. This is how, on the third day, I heard the saga of the baobabs.

Once again it was due to the sheep, for the little prince, as if seized by grave doubt, suddenly asked me:

"It is true, isn't it, that sheep eat shrubs?"

"Yes. It's true."

"Ah! I am glad!"

I couldn't understand why it was so important that sheep should eat shrubs. But the little prince added:

"So presumably they eat baobabs as well?"

I pointed out to the little prince that baobabs are not shrubs, but trees as tall as churches, and that, even if he took with him a whole herd of elephants, that herd would not get to the end of a single baobab.

The idea of a herd of elephants made the little prince laugh: "You'd have to stack them on top of one another…"

But he added wisely:

"Baobabs, before they grow big, start out little."

"True enough! But why do you want your sheep to eat little baobabs?"

He answered: "Well! Obviously!" as if it was self-evident. And I had to make a big mental effort to think the problem through on my own.

True enough, on the little prince's planet as on all planets, there were useful plants and weeds. And consequently, the useful seeds of useful plants and the noxious seeds of weeds. But the seeds are invisible. They sleep secretly in the earth until it takes the fancy of one of them to wake up. Then it stretches and pushes out towards the sun, timidly at first, a ravishing, harmless little

shoot. If the shoot belongs to a radish or a rose, you can let it grow as it pleases. But if it's a weed, you must uproot the plant the moment you identify it. Now there were some terrible seeds on the little prince's planet… they were baobab seeds. The planet's soil was infested with them.

And if you wait too long with a baobab, you can never get rid
of it. It takes up the whole planet. It pierces it with its roots.
And if the planet is too small, and the baobabs too many, they
break it apart.

"It's a question of discipline," the little prince told me later.
"Once you've scrubbed up in the morning, you must take care
to scrub up the planet. You have to apply yourself regularly to
the task of grubbing up baobabs as soon as you can distinguish

them from the roses they so resemble when young. It's a very tedious job, but very straightforward."

One day he advised me to attempt a beautiful drawing that would really bring it home to children from my world: "If ever they go travelling," he told me, "it could come in useful. Sometimes it's harmless to put off a task. But in the case of baobabs, it's always disastrous. I knew a planet on which a lazy person lived. He'd ignored three saplings…"

As instructed by the little prince, I drew the planet in question. I don't like to take a moralizing tone. But the danger posed by baobabs is so little known, and so great are the risks to anyone who stumbles onto an asteroid, that for once I set aside my reservations. I say: "Children! Beware of baobabs!" It's to warn my friends who, like me, have for so long flirted with danger without realizing it, that I have worked so hard on this drawing. The lesson it imparts was worth the effort. You may well ask: why aren't there other drawings as grandiose in this book as the drawing of baobabs? The answer is very simple: I've tried but I haven't managed. When I drew the baobabs I was filled with a sense of urgency.

The baobabs.

VI

Ah, little prince, so I learnt, bit by bit, about your melancholy little life. For a long time your only distraction had been the beauty of sunsets. I learnt this new detail on the fourth morning, when you said to me:

"I love sunsets. Let's go and see a sunset…"

"Well you have to wait…"

"Wait for what?"

"For the sun to set."

You looked very surprised at first, and then you laughed at yourself. And you said to me:

"I still think I'm at home!"

Quite so. As everyone knows, when it's midday in the United States, the sun is setting in France. You would simply need to be able to get to France in one minute in order to watch a sunset. Unfortunately France is much too far away. But you, on your tiny planet, had only to move your chair a few paces. And you watched twilight whenever you pleased…

"One day, I saw the sun set forty-four times!"

A bit later you added:

"You know… when you're really sad you come to love sunsets…"

"That day of the forty-four sunsets, were you really so sad?"

But the little prince gave no reply.

VII

On the fifth day, thanks as ever to the sheep, this secret about the little prince's life was revealed to me. He asked me suddenly, straight out, as if it were the result of a problem long mulled over in silence:

"A sheep, if it eats shrubs, does it also eat flowers?"

"A sheep eats everything it finds."

"Even flowers that have thorns?"

"Yes. Even flowers that have thorns."

"What's the use of having thorns, then?"

I had no idea. I was very absorbed just then in trying to unscrew an over-tight bolt from my engine. I was very concerned, as my breakdown was starting to look very serious, and with drinking water running out I was fearing the worst.

"What's the use of having thorns?"

The little prince never gave up on a question once he had asked it. I was irritated by my bolt and gave any old answer:

"Thorns are of no use, flowers have them out of pure nastiness!"

"Oh!"

But after a pause he retorted, almost reproachfully:

"I don't believe you! Flowers are weak. They're naive. They do what they can to reassure themselves. They think they're fearsome with their thorns..."

I didn't answer. At that instant I was telling myself: "If this bolt continues to resist, I'll knock it out with a hammer blow." Again the little prince interrupted my thoughts:

"And you, you think that flowers—"

"No! No! I don't think anything! I just said whatever came into my head. I've serious things to attend to!"

He looked at me in astonishment.

"Serious things!"

He saw me, with my hammer in my hand, and my fingers black with engine oil, bent over an object that seemed to him very ugly.

"You speak like a grown-up!"

This made me feel a bit ashamed. Mercilessly he added:

"You're confusing everything… you're getting everything mixed up!"

He was really very annoyed. He was shaking his golden locks in the wind:

"I know a planet with a red-faced man on it. He has never smelt a flower. He has never looked at a star. He has never loved anyone. He has never done anything but sums. And all day long he repeats like you: 'I'm a serious man, I'm a serious man!' – and it makes him swell up with pride. But he's not a man, he's a mushroom!"

"A what?"

"A mushroom!"

The little prince was now quite pale with anger.

"For millions of years, flowers have produced thorns. Even so, for millions of years sheep have eaten the flowers. And don't you think it's important to want to understand why they go to such lengths to produce thorns that serve no purpose? Is the war between sheep and flowers of no consequence? Isn't it more significant and more important than the sums of a fat, red-faced man? And what if I know of a flower that's the only one of its kind in the world, that exists nowhere except on my planet, and that a little sheep could

25

destroy in one go, just like that, one fine day, without realizing what it's doing – is that of no consequence?"

He reddened, then continued:

"If someone loves a flower which is the only one of its kind in all the millions and millions of stars, that's enough for him to be happy when he looks up at them. He says to himself, 'My flower is out there somewhere…' But if the sheep eats the flower, it's as if, for him, all the stars suddenly went out. And you think that's of no consequence!"

He couldn't say any more. He began suddenly to sob. Night had fallen. I had dropped my tools. What did I care about my hammer and my bolt, about thirst and death? On a star, a planet, on my planet, here on Earth, there was a little prince who needed comforting! I took him in my arms. I rocked him. I told him: "The flower you love isn't in danger… I'll draw a muzzle for your sheep… I'll draw some armour for your flower… I'll…" I wasn't quite sure what to say. I felt very clumsy. I didn't know how to reach him, how to get back to him… What a mysterious place, the land of tears!

VIII

I came soon enough to know this flower better. On the little prince's planet there had always been very simple flowers, adorned with a single array of petals, and they took up hardly any space, and troubled no one. They appeared one morning in the grass, and faded away by nightfall. But this particular one had sprouted one day, from a seed of unknown origin, and the little prince had kept a close eye on this shoot that looked like no other. Maybe it was a new kind of baobab. But the sapling soon stopped growing, and set about preparing a flower. Witnessing the appearance of an enormous bud, the little prince felt certain that something miraculous would emerge, but the flower went on and on preparing herself to be beautiful, in the privacy of her green bedroom. She was choosing her colours with care. She was dressing herself slowly, adjusting her petals one by one. She didn't want to come out all rumpled like a poppy. She wanted to appear only in the full radiance of her beauty. Oh yes! She was very coquettish. Her mysterious toilette had lasted for days and days. And then one morning, at sunrise as it happens, she revealed herself.

And the flower, who had worked so diligently, said with a yawn:

"Ah! I'm scarcely awake… I beg your pardon… I'm all dishevelled…"

The little prince could not contain his admiration:

"How beautiful you are!"

"Aren't I?" said the flower softly. "And I was born at the same time as the sun…"

The little prince could tell that she was none too modest, but she was so touching!

"It is time, I think, for breakfast,"

27

she soon added, "would you be so kind as to think of me…"

And the little prince, having gone, all abashed, to fill a watering can with fresh water, waited on the flower.

So, with her prickly vanity, she had soon begun to torment him. One day, for instance, while talking about her four thorns, she had said to the little prince:

"Let them come, the tigers, with their claws!"

"There aren't any tigers on my planet," the little prince objected. "And besides, tigers don't eat grass."

"I am not grass," the flower replied quietly.

"Forgive me…"

"I have no fear of tigers, but I do have a horror of draughts. You wouldn't happen to have a screen?"

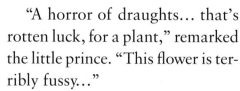

"A horror of draughts… that's rotten luck, for a plant," remarked the little prince. "This flower is terribly fussy…"

"In the evening you will put a cloche over me. Your home is very cold. It's badly set up. Where I come from…"

But she broke off. She had arrived in the form of a seed. She couldn't have known anything about other worlds. Humiliated to have let herself be caught out preparing so naive a lie, she coughed two or three times, to put the little prince in the wrong.

"About that screen?…"

"I was going to fetch it, but you were talking to me!"

All the same, she forced herself to cough in order to make him feel guilty.

Thus, in spite of his love's good intentions, the little prince had soon come to distrust her. He had taken trivial words seriously, and had become very unhappy.

"I shouldn't have listened to her," he confided to me one day, "you must never listen to flowers. You must look at them and smell them. Mine perfumed my planet, but I didn't know how to appreciate it. That nonsense about claws, which so annoyed me, ought to have softened my heart…"

He confided further:

"I got it all wrong! I should have judged her on her deeds and not on her words. She gave me fragrance and light. I should never have run away! I should have noticed the tenderness behind her feeble wiles. Flowers are so contradictory! But I was too young to know how to love her."

IX

I believe he escaped by hitching a ride with a flock of migrating wild birds. On the morning of his departure he made sure his planet was shipshape. Carefully he swept his active volcanoes. He had two active volcanoes. And this was very convenient for heating up his breakfast in the morning. He also had an extinct volcano. But, as he said: "You never know!" So he also swept the extinct volcano. Properly swept, volcanoes burn gently and reliably, without eruptions. Volcanic eruptions are like chimney fires. Obviously on our planet we are much too small to sweep our volcanoes. This is why they cause us so much trouble.

The little prince also grubbed up, a little wistfully, the last baobab shoots. He thought he would never have to return. But that morning, all these familiar tasks seemed to him ever so agreeable. And when he watered his flower for the last time, and was about to shelter her under her cloche, he found that he wanted to cry.

"Farewell," he said to the flower.

But she did not reply.

"Farewell," he said again.

The flower gave a cough. But it wasn't because of her cold.

"I've been foolish," she said to him at last. "Please forgive me. Try to be happy."

He was surprised by the lack of any reproach. He stood there utterly disconcerted, the cloche in mid-air. He couldn't understand this quiet tenderness.

Carefully he swept his active volcanoes.

"I love you, of course," said the flower. "You knew nothing about it, it was my fault. It doesn't matter. But you were as foolish as me. Try to be happy... Put that cloche away. I don't want it any more."

"But the wind—"

"My cold isn't that bad... The fresh night air will do me good. I am a flower."

"But the animals—"

"I will have to put up with a caterpillar or two if I want to experience butterflies. I hear they're so beautiful. Who else will pay me a visit? You will be so far away. As for bigger animals, I have nothing to fear. I have my claws."

And ingenuously she displayed her four thorns. Then she added:

"Don't hang about like that, it's irritating. You've decided to leave. Go."

For she did not want him to see her cry. She was such a proud flower...

X

He lived in the vicinity of Asteroids 325, 326, 327, 328, 329 and 330. So he began by paying them a visit, in search of knowledge and something to do.

On the first there lived a king. The king, dressed in ermine and royal purple, sat on a throne that was at once very simple and majestic.

"Ah! Here comes a subject!" exclaimed the king when he saw the little prince. And the little prince wondered:

"How can he recognize me if he has never seen me before?"

He didn't know that, as far as kings are concerned, the world is very simple. All people are subjects.

"Come closer so I can see you better," the king said, so proud at last to have someone to be king to.

The little prince looked about for somewhere to sit, but the planet was all taken up by the magnificent ermine cloak. So he remained standing and, as he was tired, he yawned.

"It is contrary to etiquette to yawn in the presence of a king," the monarch told him. "I forbid it."

"I can't help it," said the embarrassed little prince. "I've had a long journey and I haven't slept."

"Well then," said the king, "I command you to yawn. I haven't seen anyone yawn for years. Yawns are a novelty for me. Go on! Yawn some more. That's a command."

"It's intimidating… I can't do it…" said the little prince, blushing.

"Hum! Hum!" replied the king. "Then I… I command you sometimes to yawn and sometimes to…"

He muttered a little and seemed put out.

For above all the king required that his authority be respected. He did not tolerate disobedience. He was an absolute monarch. But, as he was very decent, he gave reasonable orders.

As he commonly remarked, "If I ordered a general to change into a seabird, and the general did not obey, it would not be the general's fault. It would be my fault."

"May I sit?" enquired the little prince shyly.

"I command you to sit," replied the king, majestically gathering in part of his ermine cloak.

But the little prince was surprised. The planet was tiny. What could the king possibly rule over?

"Sire," he said to him, "I beg your pardon for asking—"

"I command you to ask," said the king hastily.

"Sire… what do you rule over?"

"Everything," replied the king, very plainly.

"Everything?"

With a discreet gesture the king indicated his planet, the other planets and the stars.

"All of that?" said the little prince.

"All of that," replied the king.

He was not only an absolute monarch, but a universal one.

"And do the stars obey you?"

"Of course," said the king. "They obey at once. I will not tolerate indiscipline."

The little prince marvelled at such power. If he had had the same for himself, he could have witnessed not forty-four, but seventy-two, or even a hundred, or even two hundred sunsets in one day, without once having to move his chair! And as he felt a little sad at the memory of his abandoned little planet, he found the courage to beg a favour of the king:

"I would like to see a sunset… Do me this pleasure… Command the sun to set…"

"If I commanded a general to fly from one flower to another like a butterfly, or to write a tragedy, or to change himself into a seabird, and the general did not carry out my command, which of the two of us would be in the wrong?"

"It would be you," said the little prince firmly.

"Exactly. We must demand of people only what they can deliver," continued the king. "Authority rests above all on reason. If one orders one's people to throw themselves into the sea, they will stage a revolution. I have the right to command obedience because my commands are reasonable."

"What about my sunset?" renewed the little prince, who never let go of a question once he had asked it.

"You will have your sunset. I will issue the command. But I will wait, according to my principles of governance, for the moment to be favourable."

"When will that be?" asked the little prince.

"Hem! Hem!" replied the king, who began to consult a large calendar. "Hem! Hem! It will be around... around... tonight it will be around twenty to eight! And you will see how well I am obeyed."

The little prince yawned. He missed his lost sunset. Furthermore, he was a little bored already:

"I've nothing more to do here," he said to the king. "I'll be off!"

"Don't leave," replied the king, who was so proud to have a subject. "Don't leave, I'm making you a minister!"

"Minister of what?"

"Of... of Justice!"

"But there's no one to judge!"

"One never knows," said the king. "I've not yet done a tour of my kingdom. I am very old, I've no space for a carriage, and it wearies me to walk."

"Oh, but I've already seen," said the little prince, bending to glance again at the other side of the planet. "There's no one there either."

"Then you will preside in judgement over yourself," the king replied. "That's the most difficult task. It is much more difficult to judge oneself than to judge others. If you manage to judge yourself fairly, you will truly be a wise man."

"Well," said the little prince, "I can judge myself anywhere. I don't need to live here."

"Hem! Hem!" said the king, "I do believe that somewhere on my planet there is an old rat. I can hear it at night. You can judge this old rat. From time to time you can condemn it to death. Thus, its life will depend on your justice. But each time you will pardon it, in order to economize. There's only the one."

"I don't like condemning to death," said the little prince, "and I do believe I'm leaving."

"No," said the king.

But the little prince, having got himself ready, did not wish to cause the old monarch any pain:

"If His Majesty wishes to be obeyed promptly, He might give me a reasonable command. He might, for instance, order me to depart within a minute. It seems to me that the conditions are favourable…"

Since the king had made no reply, the little prince hesitated at first, and then, with a sigh, he took off…

"I make you my ambassador," the king hastened to cry after him.

He had an air of great authority.

"Grown-ups are really strange," the little prince thought to himself on his travels.

XI

A conceited man lived on the second planet. "Ah-ha! Here's an admirer who's come to see me!" the conceited man cried from afar as soon as he noticed the little prince.

To vain people, other people are always admirers.

"Hello," said the little prince. "That's a funny hat you've got."

"It's for greeting people," the conceited man replied. "It's to acknowledge when people applaud me. Unfortunately no one ever comes this way."

"Oh yes?" said the little prince, who didn't understand.

"Clap your hands," said the conceited man.

The little prince clapped his hands. The conceited man raised his hat in a modest salute.

"Well," the little prince said to himself, "it's more fun than my visit to the king." And he began again to clap his hands. Again the conceited man raised his hat in acknowledgement.

After five minutes of this the little prince grew tired of the game's monotony.

"And what must one do," he asked, "for the hat to drop?"

But the conceited man did not hear him. Vain people only ever hear praise.

"Do you really admire me a great deal?" he asked the little prince.

"What does 'admire' mean?"

"To 'admire' means to recognize that I am the handsomest, the best-dressed, the richest and the most intelligent man on the planet."

"But you're the only man on your planet!"

"Do me a favour. Admire me even so!"

"I admire you," said the little prince, with a small shrug of his shoulders, "but how can that possibly matter to you?"

And the little prince went on his way.

"Grown-ups truly are odd," he thought simply to himself on his travels.

XII

The next planet was inhabited by a drinker. This visit was very brief, but it plunged the little prince into a deep melancholy.

"What are you doing there?" he said to the drinker, whom he found seated in silence before a collection of empty bottles and a collection of full bottles.

"I'm drinking," said the drinker with a lugubrious expression.

"Why are you drinking?" the little prince asked.

"To forget," replied the drinker.

"To forget what?" wondered the little prince, feeling sorry for him already.

"To forget that I am ashamed," admitted the drinker, bowing his head.

"Ashamed of what?" asked the little prince, wanting to help him.

"Ashamed of drinking!" concluded the drinker who buried himself in silence once and for all.

And the little prince went away, bewildered.

"Grown-ups truly are very, very odd," he thought to himself on his travels.

XIII

The fourth planet belonged to a businessman. This man was so busy that he didn't even raise his head when the little prince appeared.

"Hello," said the latter. "Your cigarette has gone out."

"Three and two is five. Five and seven, twelve. Twelve and three is fifteen. Hello. Fifteen and seven is twenty-two. Twenty-two and six, twenty-eight. No time to relight it. Twenty-six and five is thirty-one. Phew! So that's five hundred and one million, six hundred and twenty-two thousand, seven hundred and thirty-one."

"Five hundred million what?"

"Eh? Are you still here? Five hundred and one million... lost it... I have so much work! I'm a serious man, I am, no time for nonsense! Two and five is seven..."

"Five hundred and one million what?" repeated the little prince, who had never in all his life given up on a question once he had asked it.

The businessman looked up:

"In my fifty-four years on this planet, I've only been interrupted three times. The first time, twenty-two years ago, it was a May bug that had dropped in from God knows where. It made a frightful noise, and I made four errors in my calculations. The second time, eleven years ago, it was a fit of rheumatism. I'm short of exercise. I don't have time to stroll about. I'm a serious man, I am. The third time… this is it. So I was saying, five hundred and one million…"

"Millions of what?"

The businessman understood that there was no chance of being left in peace:

"Millions of those little things you sometimes see in the sky."

"Flies?"

"No, no, little things that shine."

"Bees?"

"Of course not. The little golden things that make idlers wonder. But I'm a serious man, I am. I don't have time to daydream."

"Ah! Stars?"

"That's it. Stars."

"And what do you do with five hundred million stars?"

"Five hundred and one million, six hundred and twenty-two thousand, seven hundred and thirty-one. I'm a serious man, I am, I'm precise."

"And what do you do with these stars?"

"What do I do with them?"

"Yes."

"Nothing. I own them."

"You own the stars?"

"Yes."

"But I've already seen a king who—"

"Kings don't own. They 'rule' over. It's quite different."

"And what's the point of owning the stars?"

"The point is to be rich."

"And what's the point of being rich?"

"So you can buy other stars, if someone discovers any."

"This one," the little prince said to himself, "reasons a little bit like my drunkard."

Even so he continued to ask questions:

"How can anyone own the stars?"

"Who do they belong to?" replied the businessman crankily.

"I don't know. To nobody."

"Then they're mine, because I thought of it first."

"Is that all it takes?"

"Of course. When you find a diamond that doesn't belong to anyone, it's yours. When you find an island that doesn't belong to anyone, it's yours. When you're the first to have an idea, you get it patented: it's yours. And I own the stars, since no one before me ever thought of owning them."

"That's true," said the little prince. "And what do you do with them?"

"I manage them. I count them and count them again," said the businessman. "It's difficult. But I'm a serious man!"

The little prince was still not satisfied.

"For my part, if I own a scarf, I can put it round my neck and take it with me. If I own a flower, I can pick my flower and take it with me. But you can't pick the stars."

"No, but I can put them in a bank."

"What does that mean?"

"It means I write the number of my stars on a small piece of paper. And then I lock up this piece of paper in a drawer."

"And that's all?"

"That's enough!"

"It's amusing," thought the little prince. "It's quite poetic. But it isn't very serious."

The little prince had very different notions of what was serious from the notions of grown-ups.

"Personally I have a flower," he continued, "which I water every day. I have three volcanoes that I sweep every week. Because I also sweep the one that's extinct. You never know. It's useful for my volcanoes, and it's useful for my flower, that I own them. But you're of no use to the stars..."

The businessman opened his mouth but could think of no answer, and the little prince went away.

"Grown-ups truly are utterly extraordinary," he thought simply to himself on his travels.

XIV

The fifth planet was very odd. It was the smallest of the lot. There was just room for a streetlamp and a lighter of streetlamps. The little prince could not begin to understand what purpose a streetlamp and a lighter of streetlamps might serve, somewhere out in space, on a planet without houses or inhabitants. Even so he said to himself:

"It may well be that this man is absurd. And yet he's less absurd than the king, the conceited man, the businessman and the drinker. At least there's some point to his work. When he lights his street-lamp, it's as if he brings another star into being, or a flower. When he puts out the lamp, the flower or the star go to sleep. It's a very beautiful occupation. It's genuinely useful because it's beautiful."

When he landed on the planet, he greeted the lamplighter respectfully:

"Hello. Why have you just put out your lamp?"

"It's my job," replied the lamplighter. "Good morning."

"What is your job?"

"It's to put out my lamp. Good evening."

And he lit it again.

"But then why have you just lit it again?"

"It's my job," replied the lamplighter.

"I don't understand," said the little prince.

"There's nothing to understand," said the lamplighter. "A job is a job. Good morning."

And he put out his streetlamp.

Then he mopped his brow with a red-chequered handkerchief.

"This is terrible work. It was all right in the past. I put the light out in the morning and I lit up at night. I had the rest of the day to relax, and the rest of the night to sleep…"

"And, since that time, your job has changed?"

"The job hasn't changed," said the lamplighter. "That's just the trouble! Year on year the planet's been spinning ever faster, and the job hasn't changed!"

"This is terrible work."

"So?" said the little prince.

"So now it revolves once a minute, I don't get a second's rest. I light up and put out once every minute!"

"That is funny! Your days last one minute!"

"It's not funny at all," said the lamplighter. "We've been talking to each other for a month already."

"A month?"

"Right. Thirty minutes. Thirty days! Good evening."

And he relit his streetlamp.

The little prince watched him and felt affection for this lamplighter who was so dedicated to his job. He remembered the sunsets which he himself used to go looking for, taking his chair with him. He wanted to help his friend:

"You know… I know a way for you to rest whenever you want to…"

"I always want to," said the lamplighter.

For it's possible to be, at one and the same time, dedicated and lazy.

The little prince continued:

"Your planet is so small that you can go around it in three strides. You have only to walk slowly enough to stay constantly in the sun. When you want to rest you walk… and the day will last as long as you please."

"That doesn't help me much," said the lamplighter. "What I like in life is sleeping."

"That's bad luck," said the little prince.

"It's bad luck," said the lamplighter. "Good morning."

And he put out his streetlamp.

"That man," said the little prince to himself as he continued on his travels, "that man would be despised by all the others, by the king, the conceited man, the drinker and the businessman. And yet he's the only one who doesn't strike me as ridiculous. Perhaps it's because he takes care of something other than himself."

He gave a regretful sigh and thought to himself moreover:

"He's the only one who could have become my friend. But his planet really is too small. There isn't room for two…"

What the little prince didn't dare admit to himself was that he missed this blessed planet, above all, on account of its one thousand four hundred and forty sunsets every twenty-four hours!

XV

The sixth planet was ten times larger. It was the home of an old man who wrote enormous books.

"I say! There's an explorer!" he cried when he saw the little prince.

The little prince sat on the table and gave himself a moment. He had already done so much travelling!

"Where have you come from?" the old man said to him.

"What is this big book?" said the little prince. "What do you do here?"

"I am a geographer," said the old man.

"What's a geographer?"

"He is an expert who knows the location of seas, rivers, cities, mountains and deserts."

"That *is* interesting," said the little prince. "At last a real profession!" And he looked around at the geographer's planet. He had never yet seen a planet so magnificent.

"Your planet is very beautiful. Are there oceans?"

"I have no idea," said the geographer.

"Ah!" (The little prince was disappointed.) "What about mountains?"

"I have no idea," said the geographer.

"And cities and rivers and deserts?"

"I have no idea either," said the geographer.

"But you're a geographer!"

"Indeed so," said the geographer, "but I am not an explorer. I desperately lack explorers. It isn't the geographer's job to tally cities, rivers, mountains, seas, oceans and deserts. A geographer is too important to go strolling about. He never leaves his study. But he invites explorers in. He asks them questions, and records their recollections. And if the recollections of one of them seem interesting to him, the geographer investigates the explorer's morals."

"Why's that?"

"Because an explorer who would tell lies would have a catastrophic effect on geography books. As would an explorer who drinks too much."

"Why's that?" said the little prince.

"Because drunkards see double. And so the geographer would record two mountains where there is only one."

"I know someone," said the little prince, "who would make a bad explorer."

"Quite possibly. So, when the explorer's morals appear to be sound, one investigates his discovery."

"You go and see?"

"No. That's too complicated. Rather one insists that the explorer provide proof. If for instance we're talking about the discovery of a large mountain, one insists that he bring back some large stones."

Suddenly the geographer became excited.

"But you come from afar! You are an explorer! You will describe your planet to me!"

And the geographer, having opened up his register, sharpened his pencil. First one notes down an explorer's account in pencil. Only when the explorer has provided proof does one write in ink.

"Well?" asked the geographer.

"Oh!" said the little prince. "My place isn't that interesting – it's very small. I have three volcanoes. Two active volcanoes and one extinct. Though you never know."

"You never know," said the geographer.

"I also have a flower."

"We make no note of flowers," said the geographer.

"Why ever not! There's nothing prettier!"

"Because flowers are ephemeral."

"What does 'ephemeral' mean?"

"Geography books," said the geographer, "are the most serious of all books. They never go out of date. It's very rare for a mountain to change location. It's very rare for an ocean to empty of its water. We write down things that are eternal."

"But extinct volcanoes can come back to life," interrupted the little prince. "What does 'ephemeral' mean?"

"Whether volcanoes are active or extinct, it's all the same to us," said the geographer. "What matters for us is the mountain. That never changes."

"But what does 'ephemeral' mean?" repeated the little prince, who had never in his life given up on a question once he had asked it.

"It means 'threatened with imminent extinction'."

"My flower is threatened with imminent extinction?"

"Naturally."

"My flower is ephemeral," the little prince said to himself, "and she has only four thorns to defend herself against the world! And I've left her all alone at home!"

This was his first experience of regret. But he took courage:

"Where do you recommend I visit?" he asked.

"Planet Earth," the geographer replied. "It has a good reputation…"

And off the little prince went, thinking about his flower.

XVI

The seventh planet, then, was Earth.

Earth isn't any old planet! It boasts a hundred and eleven kings (not forgetting, of course, African chieftains), seven thousand geographers, nine hundred thousand businessmen, seven and a half million drunkards, three hundred and eleven million vain people – all told, about two billion grown-ups.

To give you an idea of Earth's dimensions, I will tell you that before the invention of electricity it was necessary, across the six continents, to maintain a veritable army of four hundred and sixty-two thousand five hundred and eleven lamplighters.

From a distance the effect was splendid. The movements of this army were regulated like those of a ballet company. First it was the turn of the lamplighters of New Zealand and Australia. Then these, having lit their lamps, went off to sleep. Into the dance came the lamplighters of China and Siberia. Then they too were conjured away into the wings. Next it was the turn of the lamplighters of Russia and the Indies. Then those of Africa and Europe. Then those of South America. Then those of North America. And not once did they mix up the order of their entrances on stage. It was grandiose.

Only the lighter of the one streetlamp at the North Pole and his colleague of the one streetlamp at the South Pole led lives of idleness and ease: they worked twice a year.

XVII

Sometimes, when you're trying to be witty, it can happen that you fib a little. I haven't been entirely honest in telling you about the lamplighters. I'm in danger of giving a false impression of our planet to those who don't know it. Humans occupy very little space on Earth. If the Earth's two billion inhabitants stood together, packed a bit tightly, as if at a meeting, they would fit easily into a public square twenty miles long by twenty miles wide. One could cram humanity onto the very smallest Pacific island.

Grown-ups, of course, will not believe you. They think they take up lots of space. They believe themselves to be as substantial as baobabs. You will advise them, then, to do their sums. They love figures: it will make them happy. But don't waste your time on this chore. It's unnecessary. Trust me.

The little prince, then, having arrived on Earth, was most surprised not to see anyone. He was beginning to worry that he'd got the wrong planet, when a coil the colour of the moon stirred in the sand.

"Good evening," said the little prince tentatively.

"Good evening," said the snake.

"What planet have I landed on?" asked the little prince.

"On Earth, in Africa," replied the snake.

"Ah!... Are there no people on Earth, then?"

"This is the desert. There's nobody in the deserts. The Earth is big," said the snake.

The little prince sat on a stone and looked up at the sky:

"I wonder," he said, "if the stars shine so that everyone can one day find their own again. Look at my planet. It's right above us... But how far away it is!"

"It's beautiful," said the snake. "What brings you here?"

"I have some troubles with a flower," said the little prince.

"Ah!" said the snake.

And they were both silent.

"Where are the people?" the little prince continued at last. "It's a bit lonely in the desert..."

"It's also lonely among people," said the snake.

The little prince looked at him for a long time:

"What a funny creature you are," he said at last, "as thin as a finger."

"But I am more powerful than the finger of a king," said the snake.

The little prince smiled:

"You're not all that powerful... you don't even have legs... you can't even travel..."

"I can take you farther away than any boat," said the snake.

It curled itself around the little prince's ankle, like a golden bracelet.

"Whoever I touch, I return to the ground whence they came," it continued. "But you are pure and come from a star..."

The little prince gave no reply.

"I feel sorry for you, you so weak, on this Earth of granite. I can help you one day if you miss your planet too much. I can—"

"What a funny creature you are," he said at last,
"as thin as a finger."

"Oh! I've understood well enough," said the little prince, "but why do you always talk in riddles?"

"I solve them all," said the snake.

And they were both silent.

XVIII

The little prince walked across the desert and encountered only one flower. A flower with three petals, an insignificant flower...

"Hello," said the little prince.

"Hello," said the flower.

"Where are the people?" the little prince asked politely.

The flower had once seen a caravan go by.

"People? I believe there are six or seven of them. I glimpsed them years ago. But you never know where to find them. The wind blows them about. They lack roots – it's most troubling for them."

"Farewell," said the little prince.

"Farewell," said the flower.

XIX

The little prince climbed a tall mountain. The only mountains he had ever known were the three volcanoes that came up to his knees. And he used the extinct volcano as a stool. "From a mountain as high as this," he told himself, "I'll be able to see the whole planet and all the people in one go." But he saw only sharpened needles of rock.

"Hello," he said, trying his luck.

"Hello... Hello... Hello..." replied the echo.

"Who are you?" said the little prince.

"Who are you... who are you... who are you..." replied the echo.

"Be my friends, I'm alone," he said.

"I'm alone... I'm alone... I'm alone," replied the echo.

"What a strange planet," he now thought. "It's all dry and pointy and salty. And people have no imagination. They repeat what you say to them... Back home I had a flower: she was always the first to speak..."

XX

Having walked a long time through sandy wastes, rocks and snows, it happened that the little prince came upon a road. And all roads lead to people.

"Hello," he said.

It was a garden full of roses.

"Hello," said the roses.

The little prince looked at them. They all looked like his flower.

"Who are you?" he asked them in astonishment.

"We are roses," said the roses.

"Ah!" said the little prince.

And he felt very miserable. His flower had told him that she was alone of her kind in the universe. And here there were five thousand, all alike, in just one garden!

"She would be most upset," he told himself, "if she saw this... She would cough heavily and pretend to die to escape the ridicule. And what choice would I have but to pretend to look after her; or else, to humiliate me too, she really would let herself die..."

"This planet is all dry and pointy and salty."

Then he said to himself: "I thought I was blessed with a unique flower, and I only have an ordinary rose. That and my three, knee-high volcanoes, one of which is probably extinct for ever, don't make me much of a prince..." And, lying in the grass, he wept.

<h1 style="text-align:center">XXI</h1>

At this moment the fox appeared:

"Hello," said the fox.

"Hello," replied the little prince politely, turning around but seeing nothing.

"I'm here," said the voice, "under the apple tree..."

"Who are you?" said the little prince. "You *are* pretty."

"I'm a fox," said the fox.

"Come and play with me," the little prince asked him. "I am so sad…"

"I can't play with you," said the fox. "I've not been tamed."

"Ah! Sorry," said the little prince.

But after thinking about it, he added:

"What does 'tame' mean?"

"You're not from these parts," said the fox. "What are you looking for?"

"I'm looking for people," said the little prince. "What does 'tame' mean?"

"People," said the fox, "have guns and go hunting. It's so inconvenient! They also raise chickens. It's all they're good for. Are you looking for chickens?"

"No," said the little prince, "I'm looking for friends. What does 'tame' mean?"

"It's something too well forgotten," said the fox. "It means 'to forge bonds...'"

"Forge bonds?"

"Of course," said the fox. "As far as I'm concerned, you're just another little boy, no different from a hundred thousand other little boys. I don't need you. And you don't need me either. As far as you're concerned, I'm just a fox like a hundred thousand other foxes. But if you tame me, we'll need one another. You will be unique in the world for me. I will be unique in the world for you..."

"I'm beginning to understand," said the little prince. "There's this flower... I think she tamed me."

"It's possible," said the fox. "You see all sorts on Earth..."

"Oh! This isn't on Earth," said the little prince.

The fox seemed most intrigued:

"On another planet?"

"Yes."

"There are hunters on this planet?"

"No."

"Now that's interesting! And chickens?"

"No."

"Nothing's perfect," sighed the fox.

But the fox returned to his idea:

"My life is monotonous. I chase chickens, men chase me. All chickens look alike, and all men look alike. No wonder I get a bit bored. But if you tame me, it'll be as if my life is filled with sunlight. I'll know a sound of footsteps that will be different from all others. Other footsteps make me run for shelter. Yours will call me out of my burrow, like music. And then look! You see, over there, those fields of wheat? I don't eat bread. Wheat's useless to me. Fields of wheat don't remind me of anything. And that's sad! But you have golden hair. So it will be marvellous when you have tamed me! Wheat, being golden, will remind me of you. And I will love the sound of the wind in the wheat…"

The fox went quiet and watched the little prince for a long time:

"Please… tame me!" he said.

"Gladly," replied the little prince, "but I don't have much time. I have friends to find and lots of things to learn."

"We can only know the things we tame," said the fox. "Men no longer have time to get to know anything. They buy things readymade from the shops. But since there aren't any shops that sell friends, men no longer have friends. If it's a friend you want, tame me!"

"What must I do?" said the little prince.

"You have to be very patient," replied the fox. "First you'll sit a little way from me, like this, in the grass. I'll watch you in the corner of my eye and you'll say nothing. Language leads to misunderstandings. But, each day, you'll be able to sit a little closer…"

The little prince returned the next day.

"It would have been better to have come back at the same time," said the fox. "If, for instance, you come at four o'clock in the afternoon, I will start to be happy from three o'clock. The closer the time comes, the happier I will be. As soon as it's four o'clock, I'll get restless and worried: I'll discover the price of happiness. But if you come at any old time, I won't ever know at what time to ready my heart... There have to be rituals."

"What's a ritual?" said the little prince.

"It's something else that's been too well forgotten," said the fox. "It's what makes one day different from other days, one hour from other hours. The men who hunt me, for instance, have a ritual. On Thursdays they go dancing with the girls of the village. And so Thursday is a wonderful day! I go strolling all the way to the vineyard. If the hunters went dancing at any old time, the days would all be the same, and I would have no holidays."

And so the little prince tamed the fox. And when it was nearly time for them to part:

"Ah!" said the fox. "I shall cry."

"It's your fault," said the little prince. "I didn't mean you any harm, but you wanted me to tame you..."

"Of course," said the fox.

"But you're going to cry!" said the little prince.

"Of course," said the fox.

"If, for instance, you come at four o'clock in the afternoon,
I will start to be happy from three o'clock."

"So how has it been worth it?"

"It's been worth it," said the fox, "for the colour of wheat." Then he added:

"Go and see the roses again. You'll understand that yours is the only one of its kind in the world. You'll come back to say goodbye, and I will give you a secret as a gift."

The little prince went off to see the roses:

"You're nothing at all like my rose, you're not anything yet," he said to them. "No one has tamed you and you haven't tamed anyone. You're like my fox used to be. He was just a fox like a hundred thousand other foxes. But I made him my friend, and now he's the only one of his kind in the world."

And the roses were most put out.

"You're pretty, but you're empty," he said to them further. "No one could die for you. To an ordinary passer-by, of course, my own rose would look no different. But she on her own is more important than all of you, because she's the one I've watered. Because she's the one I put under a cloche. Because she's the one I sheltered with a screen. Because she's the one for whom I killed caterpillars (apart from two or three, for the butterflies). Because she's the one I listened to complaining, or boasting, or even sometimes being silent. Because she is my rose."

And, lying in the grass, he wept.

And he went back to the fox:

"Farewell," he said.

"Farewell," said the fox. "Here's my secret. It's very simple: you can only see clearly with your heart. What's essential is invisible to the eye."

"What's essential is invisible to the eye," the little prince repeated, so that he would remember.

"It's the time that you gave to your rose that makes your rose so important."

"It's the time that I gave to my rose…" said the little prince, so that he would remember.

"People have forgotten this truth," said the fox. "But you mustn't forget it. You become responsible for ever for what you have tamed. You are responsible for your rose…"

"I am responsible for my rose…" the little prince repeated, so that he would remember.

XXII

"Hello," said the little prince.

"Hello," said the railway switchman.

"What is it you do here?" said the little prince.

"I sort out passengers, in bunches of a thousand," said the switchman. "I send off the trains that carry them away, sometimes to the right, sometimes to the left." And an express train, lit up and rumbling like thunder, made the switchman's cabin tremble.

"They certainly are in a hurry," said the little prince. "What is it they're looking for?"

"Even the engine driver doesn't know that," said the switchman.

And a second lit-up express train rumbled past in the opposite direction.

"They're coming back already?" asked the little prince…

"They're not the same ones," said the switchman. "It's an exchange."

"Were they not happy where they were?"

"No one's ever happy where they are," said the switchman.

And a third lit-up express rumbled its thunder.

"Are they chasing the first lot of passengers?" asked the little prince.

"They're not chasing anything," said the switchman. "They're asleep in there, or yawning. Only the children press their noses against the windows."

"Only children know what they're looking for," said the little prince. "They devote themselves to a ragdoll, and it becomes very important to them, and if it gets taken away, they cry…"

"They're lucky," said the switchman.

XXIII

"Hello," said the little prince.

"Hello," said the salesman.

This was a salesmen of innovative pills for relieving thirst. You swallow one a week and no longer feel the need to drink.

"What are you selling that for?" said the little prince.

"It's a huge time-saver," said the salesman. "Experts have worked it out. It frees up fifty-three minutes per week."

"And what do you do with these fifty-three minutes?"

"You do whatever you like…"

"Personally," thought the little prince, "if I had fifty-three minutes to spend, I would walk very slowly towards a fountain…"

XXIV

It was the eighth day of my breakdown in the desert, and I had listened to the story of the salesman while drinking the last drop from my water supply:

"Ah!" I said to the little prince. "Your recollections are all well and good, but I still haven't fixed my plane, I've nothing to drink, and I'd be happy, too, if I could walk slowly towards a fountain!"

"My friend the fox…" he said to me.

"My little man, it's no longer about the fox!"

"Why?"

"Because we're going to die of thirst…"

He didn't understand what I meant, and replied:

"It's good to have had a friend, even if you're going to die. Personally, I'm very glad to have had a fox for a friend…"

"He has no sense of danger," I told myself. "He's never thirsty or hungry. A bit of sun is all he needs…"

But he was looking at me and answered my thoughts:

"I'm thirsty too… let's go and find a well…"

I made a weary gesture: it's absurd to look for a well, at random, in the immensity of the desert. Nonetheless, we set off on foot.

After we had been walking for hours, in silence, night fell, and the stars began to shine. I was seeing them as if in a dream, for I was a little feverish with thirst. The words of the little prince were dancing in my memory:

"So you are thirsty too?" I asked him.

But he didn't answer my question. He told me simply:

"Water can also be good for the heart…"

I didn't understand his answer, but I said nothing… I knew by now not to ask him questions.

He was tired. He sat down. I sat next to him. And, after a silence, he began again:

"The stars are beautiful because of a flower we cannot see…"

"Of course," I replied, and looked without speaking at the folds of sand in the moonlight.

"The desert's beautiful," he added…

And this was true. I've always loved the desert. You sit on a sand dune. You see nothing. You hear nothing. And yet there's something glimmering in the silence...

"What makes the desert beautiful," said the little prince, "is that it's concealing a well somewhere..."

I was surprised to understand all of a sudden the mysterious glimmer of the sand. When I was a little boy, I lived in an old house, and according to legend a treasure was buried there. Of course, no one had ever managed to find it, maybe no one had even looked for it. But it made the whole house feel enchanted. My house kept a secret deep in its heart...

"Yes," I said to the little prince, "whether it's a house, the stars or the desert, what makes them beautiful is invisible!"

"I'm glad," he said, "that you agree with my fox."

As the little prince was falling asleep, I took him in my arms, and set off again. I was moved. I felt I was carrying a fragile treasure. Indeed, I felt there was nothing more fragile on Earth. By the light of the moon I looked at that pale forehead, those closed eyes, those locks of hair that trembled in the wind, and I said to myself: "What I'm looking at is only a husk. What matters most is invisible..."

And as his parted lips sketched a half-smile, I told myself further: "What moves me so deeply about this sleeping little prince is his loyalty to a flower, it's the image of a rose that shines within him like the flame of a lamp, even when he's sleeping..." And he seemed to me more fragile still. You have to protect lamps: one gust of wind can blow them out...

And, walking thus, I found the well at daybreak.

He laughed, touched the rope, worked the pulley.

XXV

"People," the little prince said, "cram themselves into express trains, but they don't know what they're looking for. So they get restless and go round in circles…"

And he added:

"There's no need…"

The well we had come to did not resemble those of the Sahara. Saharan wells are simple holes dug in the sand. This one looked like a village well. But there was no village, and I thought I was dreaming.

"It's strange," I said to the little prince. "Everything is ready: the pulley, the bucket and the rope…"

He laughed, touched the rope, worked the pulley.

And the pulley creaked as an old weathervane creaks when the wind has slept for a long time.

"Can you hear?" said the little prince, "we're waking this well and it's singing…"

I didn't want him to strain himself.

"Let me do it," I said to him. "It's too heavy for you."

Slowly I heaved the bucket to the coping. I balanced it carefully. The song of the pulley still resonated in my ears and, in the water that still trembled, I saw the trembling of the sun.

"I'm thirsty for this water," said the little prince. "Give me some of it to drink…"

And I understood what he had been looking for!

I lifted the bucket to his lips. He drank, with his eyes closed.

It was sweet like a celebration. This water was much more than nutrition. It was made of the walk under the stars, of the pulley's song, of the strain of my arms. It was good for the heart, like a present. In the same way, when I was a little boy, the light of the Christmas tree, the music of Midnight Mass, the kindness in people's smiles charged my Christmas present with radiance.

"The people of your world," said the little prince, "grow five thousand roses in a single garden... and they can't find there what they are looking for..."

"They can't find it," I replied.

"And yet what they are looking for might be found in a single rose or a little water..."

"Of course," I replied.

And the little prince added:

"But eyes are blind. You must search with your heart."

I had drunk. I was breathing easily. The sand, at daybreak, is the colour of honey. This honey colour also made me happy. Why did I have to feel a sense of sadness?...

"You have to keep your promise," said the little prince to me softly, having sat down beside me again.

"What promise?"

"You know... the muzzle for my sheep... I'm responsible for that flower!"

I took my sketches out of my pocket. The little prince saw them and said, laughing:

"Your baobabs, they look a bit like cabbages..."

"Oh!"

I had been so proud of my baobabs!

"Your fox... his ears... they look a bit like horns... and they're too long!"

And he laughed some more.

"You're unfair, little man: I only knew how to draw open and closed boa constrictors."

"Oh! It will do," he said. "Children understand."

So I drew a muzzle. And I had a heavy heart as I gave it to him:

"You have plans I don't know about..."

But he didn't answer. He said to me:

"You know, my fall to Earth... tomorrow will be its anniversary..."

Then, after a silence, he continued:

"I came down very near here..."

And he blushed.

And once again, without knowing why, I felt a strange sorrow. Meanwhile a question occurred to me:

"So it wasn't by chance, the morning I met you, eight days ago, that you were walking about like that, all alone, a thousand miles from any human dwelling! You were going back to the place where you landed?"

The little prince blushed again.

And I went on, hesitantly:

"On account, perhaps, of the anniversary?..."

Once more the little prince blushed. He never answered questions, but when one blushes, it means "yes", doesn't it?

"Ah!" I said to him. "I'm afraid…"

But he said to me:

"You must get back to work now. You must go back to your machine. I'll wait for you here. Come back tomorrow evening…"

But I didn't feel reassured. I remembered the fox. You run the risk of crying a little when you've let yourself be tamed…

XXVI

Next to the well, there was the ruin of an old stone wall. Coming back from my labours the following evening, I saw from a distance my little prince sitting at the top, with his legs dangling. And I could hear him talking:

"You really don't remember?" he was saying. "It wasn't exactly here!"

Another voice must have answered him, since he replied:

"Yes! Yes! It's the day all right, but this isn't the place…"

I continued walking towards the wall. I still couldn't see or hear anyone. Even so the little prince replied again:

"…Of course. You'll see where my tracks begin in the sand. All you have to do is wait for me. I'll be there tonight."

I was twenty metres from the wall and still saw nothing.

The little prince said again, after a pause:

"You've got good venom? You're sure you won't make me suffer for long?"

I froze, my heart pounding, but still I couldn't understand.

79

"Now go away…" he said. "I want to come back down."

At that moment I too looked at the foot of the wall, and gave a start! There it was, rearing up at the little prince, one of those yellow snakes that finishes you off in thirty seconds. Even as I reached into my pocket for my revolver, I began to run, but the snake, at the noise I was making, trickled softly into the sand, like a faltering jet of water, and, without great haste, inched its way into the stones with a soft metallic sound.

I reached the wall just in time to catch my little man of a prince, as pale as snow, in my arms.

"What's all this about! You talk to snakes now!"

I had untied his trusty gold scarf. I had moistened his temples and given him to drink. And now I didn't dare ask him anything more. He looked at me solemnly and wrapped his arms about my neck. I could feel the beating of his heart like that of a dying bird that one has shot with a rifle. He said to me:

"I'm glad that you've found what was missing from your machine. You'll be able to go home…"

"How did you know?"

I was on my way to tell him that, against all odds, I had succeeded in my task!

He gave no answer to my question, but added:

"I, too, am going home today…"

Then, wistfully, he said:

"It's much farther away… it's much more difficult…"

I sensed that something extraordinary was happening. I held him like a little child in my arms, and yet it seemed to me that

"Now go away…" he said. "I want to come back down."

he was slipping straight down into an abyss and I could do nothing to keep him back...

His stare was serious, lost far away:

"I have your sheep. And the sheep's crate. And I have the muzzle..."

And he smiled wistfully.

I waited a long time. I sensed that he was warming up little by little:

"Little man, you've had a fright..."

Of course he had been frightened! But he laughed softly:

"I'll be much more frightened tonight..."

Once more my blood ran cold with a sense of the irreversible. And I realized that I couldn't bear the idea of never hearing that laugh again. For me it was like a fountain in the desert.

"Little man, I want to hear you laugh again..."

But he said to me:

"It will be a year tonight. My star will be just over the spot where I landed last year..."

"Little man, tell me it's a bad dream, this stuff about a snake and a meeting and a star..."

But he didn't answer my question. He said to me:

"What's important is invisible..."

"Of course..."

"It's like with the flower. If you love a flower which lives on a star, it's sweet, at night, to look up at the sky. All the stars are in bloom."

"Of course..."

"It's like with the water. The water you gave me to drink was like music, because of the pulley and the rope... you remember... it was good..."

"Of course..."

"You'll look at the stars at night. My place is too small to show you mine. It's better this way. For you, my star will be one of the stars. And so you will love to look at all the stars... They will all be your friends. And then I'm going to give you this gift..."

He laughed again.

"Ah! Little man, little man, I love to hear that laugh!"

"Precisely, that will be my gift... it will be like with the water..."

"What do you mean?"

"The stars are different for different people. To some, those who travel, the stars are guides. To others they are just little lights. To others, who are scientists, they are problems. To my businessman they were gold. But all of those stars are silent. You, you will have stars unlike anyone else's..."

"What do you mean?"

"When you look at the sky, at night, because I will be living on one of them, because I will be laughing on one of them, it will be for you as if all the stars are laughing. So you will have stars that know how to laugh!"

And he laughed some more.

"And once you've cheered up (we always cheer up), you will feel happy to have known me. You will always be my friend. You'll want to laugh with me. And sometimes you'll open your window, just for the pleasure of it... And your friends will be surprised to see you laughing as you look at the sky. Then you'll tell them: 'It's true, the stars always make me laugh.' And they'll think you're mad. I'll have played a wicked trick on you…"

And he laughed some more.

"It will be as if, instead of stars, I'd given you lots of little bells that can laugh…"

And he laughed some more. Then he grew serious again:

"Tonight… you know… don't come."

"I won't leave you."

"It will look like I'm in pain… it will look a little like I'm dying. That's how it is. Don't come to see that, there's no point…"

"I won't leave you."

But he was worried.

"I'm telling you this… also because of the snake. He mustn't bite you… Snakes are cruel. They can bite for the fun of it…"

"I won't leave you."

But something reassured him:

"It's true they have no venom left for the second bite…"

That night I did not see him set off. He'd got away without a sound. When I managed to catch up with him he was walking decisively, with quick strides. He merely said to me:

"Ah! There you are…"

And he took my hand. But he started to worry again:

"You've made a mistake. You'll get hurt. I will look dead, but it won't be true…"

I said nothing.

"You understand. It's too far away. I can't take this body with me. It's too heavy."

I said nothing.

"But it will be like an old abandoned husk. There's nothing sad about old husks…"

I said nothing.

He became quite discouraged. But he made another effort:

"It will be nice, you know. I too will look at the stars. All the stars will be wells with rusty pulleys. All the stars will serve me something to drink…"

I said nothing.

"It will be so funny! You'll have five hundred million little bells, I'll have five hundred million fountains…"

Then he too said nothing, for he was crying…

"There it is. Let me take a step on my own."

And he sat down, because he was frightened. He spoke again:

"You know… my flower… I'm responsible for her! And she's so feeble! And she's so naive. She has four piffling thorns to protect her against the whole world…"

I sat down because I could no longer stand. He said:
"There… That's all…"

He hesitated a little longer, then got up. He took a step forward. I could not move.

There was only a flash of yellow beside his ankle. He stood motionless for an instant. He didn't cry out. He fell softly as a tree falls. It didn't even make a sound, because of the sand.

XXVII

And now, of course, six years have passed already… I've never told this story before. When they saw me again my friends were very happy to see me alive. I was sad, but I told them: "It's tiredness…"

Now I have cheered myself up a little. Which is to say… not quite. But I know very well that he has got back to his planet, for at dawn I could not find his body. It was not such a heavy body… And I like to listen to the stars at night. It's like five hundred million little bells…

But something extraordinary has happened. The muzzle that I drew for the little prince, I forgot to add the leather strap! He will never have been able to attach it to the sheep. And so I ask myself: "What has happened on his planet? Maybe the sheep has eaten the flower…"

Sometimes I say to myself: "Surely not! The little prince shuts away his flower every night under her glass cloche, and he keeps

He fell softly as a tree falls.

a watch on his sheep..." And then I am happy. And all the stars laugh softly.

At other times I tell myself: "Everyone gets distracted once in a while, and that's all it takes! One evening he forgot the glass cloche, or else the sheep got out in the night without a sound..." At those moments the little bells turn into tears!...

This truly is a great mystery. For you who also love the little prince, as for me, nothing in the universe is the same if somewhere, who knows where, a sheep that we don't know has, or has not, eaten a rose...

Look at the sky. Ask yourself: "Has the sheep eaten or not eaten the flower?" And you will see how everything changes...

And no grown-up will ever understand how important it is!

This, for me, is the loveliest and the saddest landscape in the world. It's the same landscape as on the previous page, but I've drawn it once more to show it to you properly. This is where the little prince appeared on Earth, then disappeared.

Look at this landscape carefully so that you can be sure to recognize it, if ever you're travelling in Africa, in the desert. And if you happen to pass this way, I beg you, don't be in a hurry, wait a little just beneath the star! If at that moment a child comes to you, if he laughs, if he has golden hair, if he doesn't answer when you ask him questions, you'll know for certain who he is. Then be kind! Don't leave me feeling so sad: write quickly to tell me that he has come back…

EXTRA MATERIAL FOR YOUNG READERS

THE WRITER

The French writer Antoine de Saint-Exupéry was born on 29th June 1900 into an aristocratic family – his father and mother were a Count and Countess. His father died when he was only three, after which life was a lot less luxurious than before, but still comfortable by most people's standards. He and his mother, brother and three sisters moved into a castle shared with various aunts and cousins. He went to a Jesuit school (a strictly Catholic school) when young and then, while the First World War was raging (1914–18), to a boarding school in Switzerland with his younger brother François. In Switzerland, François became very ill with rheumatic fever, and back at home he died, with Antoine at his deathbed. The tragedy had a deep effect on Antoine, which can be seen years later in the loving but rather melancholy relationship of the narrator and the prince in *The Little Prince*.

As a young adult Antoine wasn't very successful at studying for a profession, and after giving up studies in architecture he ended up joining the army. In 1921, engaged to be married, he managed to transfer to the French Air Force, starting off as a mechanic but soon training to become a pilot. During his postings, in Morocco and France, he had quite a few crashes, and the family of his wife-to-be objected to this work, so he gave up the air force for an office job – only for the engagement to be broken off afterwards. In 1926 he started flying again, and for the next thirteen years piloted planes in many different contexts and countries, sometimes going into land-based jobs, for example as a director of an airline in Argentina, but always going back to flying.

Writing was as important to Antoine as flying. His writing was often about flying, and he even wrote *while* flying. His work started to be published in the late 1920s, but it was his 1931 book *Night Flight* – a tense tale of a pilot's disappearance in a thunderstorm – that brought him the first of many literary prizes. It was an international best-seller. His next major book wasn't published until 1939 and, with the fall of France to Nazi Germany in 1940, Antoine went into exile in America, hoping to use his influence as a celebrated author to persuade the United States to enter the war.

His wife Consuelo, whom he had married in 1931, followed him across the Atlantic. Theirs was a dramatic relationship, full of love but also stress and bust-ups. During their two years in America, Antoine produced three important books, one of which was *The Little Prince*. But he yearned to be fighting the Nazis, even though he was now eight years older than the official age limit for a pilot in the French Free Air Force, and carrying painful injuries from many past air crashes. In 1943 – after months of bureaucratic combat with the authorities – he succeeded in returning to Europe and the Free French Air Force.

Antoine's role was reconnaissance. On 31st July 1944, he took off from an airstrip in Corsica to fly a reconnaissance sortie over the Rhône Valley. He never returned. Somewhere, he crashed or was shot down – we'll probably never know which. Fifty-four years later, in 1998, a fisherman discovered his identity bracelet in the sea south of Marseille and, two years after that, fragments of his aircraft were found near to where the bracelet had been found.

THE BOOK

Only a handful of books have sold more than 100 million copies – *The Lord of the Rings* by J.R.R. Tolkien is one, and *Harry Potter and the Philosopher's Stone* by J.K. Rowling is another. A third is *The Little Prince*, a small, strange book, written in French, with quirky illustrations by the author. How and why did Antoine de Saint-Exupéry write and illustrate this unusual story?

In 1935, Antoine was competing in a race to break the air-speed record from Paris to Saigon (now called Ho Chi Minh) in Vietnam. The prize was 150,000 francs. With his navigator André Prévot, he had been in the air for nearly twenty hours when they crashed in the Sahara desert. They survived the crash, but they only had enough water for one day, and within a few days they were ill, weak, hallucinating and close to death. They were found and saved in the nick of time by a Bedouin tribesman. This life-or-death experience was one of the starting points for the writing of *The Little Prince*. The narrator finds himself in exactly the same situation, and even the little prince himself appears to have fallen out of the sky into a harsh new environment.

It was 1942 before Antoine wrote the book, however, while he was staying in America. He became one of the voices of the French resistance abroad. It was a very stressful time – he felt tormented by the suffering of France, buffeted by his tempestuous marriage to Consuelo, and he was often ill from stress, and in pain from old injuries caused by plane crashes. In these difficult conditions, he wrote half of his literary work in just a few years of his life, the most important of all being *The Little Prince*. He wrote it in a big rented house on Long Island, in the nights, often ringing up friends in the early hours on the morning to get their opinions on passages he would read out to them.

The crash in the Sahara Desert in 1935 isn't the only link between Antoine's life and the characters and events of the book. His stormy relationship with his wife Consuelo, full of energy and love but also upsets and trauma, is generally thought to be reflected in the prince's love for the rose; the prince has left the rose because she can be so haughty, proud and petulant – but beneath the strain of the relationship, she loves him and he loves her; when he is away from her, he comes to realize that they miss each other too much for him to stay away.

The blond-haired little prince himself may reflect many elements of Antoine's life. In one sense the prince is Antoine: like the author, he has travelled through the air to distant places; like the author he is on a quest to understand what life means and what is important; and like the author he has a curious mixture of simplicity, wisdom and enigma in how he examines the world. But the little prince is probably influenced by other real, blond-haired people too, from the precocious eight-year-old son of a colleague who Antoine got to know during a visit to Canada, to François, Antoine's brother who had died in childhood. When the prince in *The Little Prince* dies, somehow calm and frightened at the same time, both sad and hopeful for another life beyond the body, Antoine was clearly drawing on his memories of his brother's last hours. On his deathbed, François had said: "Don't worry. I'm all right. I can't help it. It's my body."

The Little Prince is the kind of book in which almost every character and scene may represent not just what it seems to be, but other things that Antoine is hinting at, and maybe even more things that he didn't hint at but that the reader might believe. This kind of writing, with possible hidden meanings in it, is sometimes called allegory. For example, one of the reasons the little prince has left his planet is because it is under threat from fast-growing baobab trees, and he wants to find a way of getting rid of the baobabs. Some people think that the planet represents France, the baobabs represent the invading Nazis – and the picture of the sheep that the little prince finally takes back to his planet, so that the sheep can eat the baobabs, is like America joining the war at last to help defeat the Nazis.

The illustrations in the book are by Antoine himself. He had a casual attitude to his own abilities at drawing, but his studies as an architecture student would have included detailed drawings, and throughout his life it seems he almost had as much compulsion to produce drawings as writings – and as with his writing, he often produced drawings while flying. Through repeated sketches over years, long before the book was written, the little prince gradually evolved: blond hair, turned-up nose, a long scarf and a quizzical look.

The book was extremely well received by critics when it was published, but its sales weren't spectacular at first. Antoine could only have guessed at how successful it would become – months after its publication, he was dead – but he knew in his heart that he had written a classic, and always kept a copy with him.

The book is thought to be the most translated book of fiction ever – there have been versions in over 250 languages. It is in the top five best-selling books ever, and it's interesting to realize that, like *The Lord of the Rings* and *Harry Potter and the Philosopher's Stone*, two of the other books in the top five, it is a book that is supposed to be for children but appeals to adults too, and is a book with strong elements of fantasy. There is almost no medium in which it hasn't been explored: sequels, films, TV programmes, radio plays, songs, graphic novels, musicals, anime, opera, ballet, comics... Among the most notable adaptations was an Oscar-nominated film from 1974 that turned the story into a musical comedy. In 2015 a feature-length animated film was released, in which a new character called "The Little Girl" is introduced into the enigmatic world of the crashed pilot and the little prince. It seems certain that *The Little Prince* will live on for as long as people read books.

THE CHARACTERS

The little prince

One of the two main characters in the book, the little prince is a traveller through space, searching the universe for the experience and knowledge that will enable him to return to his own little planet and care for his beloved rose. His childish-seeming innocence highlights the odd behaviours and beliefs of adults.

The narrator

The narrator is a pilot who has crashed in the Saharan Desert and needs to repair his plane before he runs out of water. Through his conversations with the prince, his understanding of what matters in life is deepened, and his ability to love is strengthened. No one has ever understood his enigmatic drawings until the little prince arrived in his life, and though they are together for only eight days and the narrator feels sad to part, he feels spiritually refreshed as well.

The rose
The rose is the one whom the little prince loves, even though she can be vain and petulant. With her bad behaviour she has more or less driven him away from the planet that they share, but inside she loves him as much as he loves her. She is under threat from the baobab trees, which grow so densely that they might suffocate her – seeking a solution to this problem is one of the reasons the prince has set off on his journey.

The fox
The fox is a wild animal who both fears people and who wants to be tamed by people, and so highlights both the risks and the pleasures of friendship. He helps the little prince to understand what matters – love – and that with love comes responsibility. The most famous quotation in the book is spoken by the fox: "Here's my secret. It's very simple: you can only see clearly with your heart. What's essential is invisible to the eye".

The king
The king occupies the first planet visited by the little prince. He is lonely, but too obsessed with the idea of being king to be interested in his visitor as an individual, or even as company – in fact, all he really wants is a subject to rule, even though he knows in his heart that no one can rule anyone unless force is used.

The conceited man

Alone on the second planet, the only thing the conceited man wants is to be admired, even if the admiration is faked rather than sincere.

The drinker

The drinker, who lives on the third planet, drinks too much alcohol because he is ashamed, and is ashamed because he drinks too much alcohol...

The businessman

The fourth planet is home to the businessman, who spends every moment counting the stars in the sky, in the belief that the more stars he counts, the more stars he owns, and the more stars he owns, the more wealth he possesses...

The lighter of streetlamps

Living on the fifth and smallest planet visited by the little prince, a planet that is spinning faster and faster as time passes, the lighter of street lamps does a very boring and pointless job which never gives him any rest. His planet used to revolve at bearable speed, but now it revolves once a minute, so as soon as he has lit the street lamps because it is getting dark, he has to extinguish them again because it is getting light...

The geographer

The sixth and biggest planet is occupied by a geographer who doesn't seem to be interested in real things, such as experiencing the world he writes about, but in reading and writing about them, and ignoring anything (such as a flower) that doesn't seem to last for ever (like a mountain).

The snake

When the little prince arrives on the Earth, the seventh and last planet that he visits, the first character he meets is the snake, who speaks in riddles. The snake is so tiny as to seem weak and powerless, but in fact has a powerful bite. It is by being bitten by the snake that the little prince dies on the Earth and, so the reader hopes and believes, reunites with his rose back on his own planet.

The railway switchman

The railway switchman sits in a cabin sending trains first to one place, then back again, trains that are packed with people who don't notice the journey and don't think about why they are repeatedly going to places and then coming back again in an endless cycle of coming and going.

The salesman

The salesman is marketing a product that stops you from being thirsty, saving you fifty-three minutes a week that you would have spent drinking water...

CLASSIC CHILDREN'S BOOKS
ILLUSTRATED BY THE AUTHORS

Antoine de Saint-Exupéry's illustrations are so distinctive, and so in keeping with his enigmatic story, that it's difficult to imagine any other illustrations being more suitable. It's fairly unusual for writers to illustrate their own books, but in the world of children's fiction there are several extremely famous examples where the harmony between the words and the pictures is as distinctive as it is in *The Little Prince*. Here are five...

Rudyard Kipling – *Just So Stories*
The English writer Rudyard Kipling (1865–1936) was a hugely famous novelist and poet whose most famous work is the children's classic *The Jungle Book*. His *Just So Stories*, published in 1902, are "origin" stories – in other words, they are fantastical accounts of how thing came about, particularly animals. In 'How the Camel Got His Hump', for example, the reader discovers that the camel was given the hump as a punishment for being idle. Other stories in the book include 'How the Elephant Got His Trunk' and 'How the Leopard Got His Spots'. Kipling wasn't as brilliant an artist as he was a writer, but his illustrations have a real poignancy to them – perhaps because, like the stories, they were produced to entertain his daughter, who tragically died three years before the book was published.

Norman Lindsay – *The Magic Pudding*
This book, subtitled *Being the Adventures of Bunyip Bluegum and his Friends Bill Barnacle and Sam Sawnoff*, is a classic of Australian's children's literature. Philip Pullman, author of the fantasy trilogy *His Dark Materials*, has described it as the funniest children's book ever written. *The Magic Pudding*, published in 1918, is thought to have been written because of an argument: someone insisted to Norman Lindsay that children like to read about fairies, while Lindsay insisted that children like to read about – well, magic puddings. In his story, the magic pudding is a pudding that always re-forms itself once eaten, so that it can be eaten again. Three friends try to keep it from the clutches of a gang called "The Pudding Thieves". Norman Lindsay (1879–1969) was a prolific Australian artist who produced a vast body of work in oils, watercolours, etchings and sculpture, so it's no surprise that his illustrations to *The Magic Pudding* are delightful.

Beatrix Potter – *The Tale of Peter Rabbit* (and other tales)
Beatrix Potter's first book, *The Tale of Peter Rabbit*, is the story of a naughty young rabbit who gets into mischief in the vegetable garden of a Scot, Mr McGregor. The book was rejected by publishers, so in 1901 Beatrix published it privately. The following year, a big publisher realized the book's potential, and Beatrix (who was born in 1866 and died in 1943) went on to write more than twenty other stories of a British countryside populated by charming animals, among them *The Tale of Squirrel Nutkin*

and *The Tale of Jemima Puddleduck*. The two things that had fascinated Beatrix most as a child were animals (she had many pets) and the art of book illustration, and the illustrations for her books developed directly from the drawings of her pets that she was forever making as a child.

TEST YOURSELF

Did you read *The Little Prince* with as much curiosity and attention as the narrator listened to the prince's strange adventures on Earth and beyond? Try this multiple-choice quiz to find out. The answers are on p. 112.

The narrator's *drawing number 1* was a picture of a boa constrictor that had swallowed an elephant. When he showed it to adults, what did they say it looked like?

    A) A steak and kidney pie
    B) A hat
    C) A map of Africa
    D) An oil slick

What does the little prince ask the narrator to draw when they first meet?

    A) A baobab tree
    B) A little princess
    C) A cow
    D) A sheep

The little prince's planet is called B 612. Who discovered B 612?

A) A French pilot
B) A Danish astronaut
C) A Turkish astronomer
D) An English aristocrat

On the first planet that the little prince visits after leaving his own planet, he meets a lonely king who has no one to rule over. What job does the king offer to the little prince in order to tempt him to stay?

A) The Sinister Minister
B) The Minister of Ministers
C) The Minister of Foolishness
D) The Minister of Justice

On the fourth planet, the little prince meets a businessman. What does the businessman count?

A) Stars
B) Money
C) Apple pips
D) Sheep

On the sixth planet, when the little prince asks the geographer what "ephemeral" means, what does the geographer reply (eventually)?

A) "It means 'promised a phenomenal meal'."
B) "It means 'threatened with imminent extinction'."
C) "It means 'offered a long sleep full of dreams'."
D) "It means 'frightened of elephant footprints'."

"Farewell," said the fox. "Here's my secret. It's very simple: you can only see clearly with your _____. What's essential is invisible to the eye"? Fill in the blank.

A) Soul
B) Spirit
C) Heart
D) Telescope

When the little prince is preparing to be bitten by a snake, so that his body can die and his soul can return to his own little planet, what does he say his body will look like?

A) An abandoned plane crashed in the desert
B) An empty crate
C) An abandoned husk
D) A snake

ANSWERS

1—B
2—D
3—C
4—D
5—A
6—B
7—C
8—C

SCORES

1 to 3 correct: Not many active volcanoes on your planet today... **4 to 6 correct:** One day you might see your rose again. **7 to 8 correct:** You *are* the little prince!

ALMA CLASSICS

ALMA CLASSICS aims to publish mainstream and lesser-known European classics in an innovative and striking way, while employing the highest editorial and production standards. By way of a unique approach the range offers much more, both visually and textually, than readers have come to expect from contemporary classics publishing.

～

To order any of our titles and for up-to-date information about our current and forthcoming publications, please visit our website on:

www.almaclassics.com

KE 09.16.